Created by
Elaine Meryl Brown, Alberto Ferreras and Chrissie Hines

Book Design by
Lisa Lloyd

Character Design by
Justin Winslow of Primal Screen

ISBN: 978-0-9828167-0-7

Printed in South Korea

El Perro y El Gato

The Dog

the Cat

Today is my birthday!

¡Hoy es mi cumpleaños!

what?

We're going to have a party!

¡Vamos a hacer una fiesta!

And I'm going to blow out the candles!

¡Y voy a soplar
las velitas!

I'm going to get lots of presents!

¡Voy a recibir muchos regalos!

¿qué?

Forget it!
I'm going to eat cake.

¡Olvídalo!
Voy a comer
pastel.

Mmmm...
I love cake.

Me gusta el pastel.

And, oh yeah...
Happy Birthday!

¡Feliz cumpleaños!

Dog **(dag)**

And **(end)**

Cat **(kat)**

Birthday **(BER-dei)**

Party **(PAR-ti)**

Candle **(KAN-del)**

What? **(¿wat?)**

Happy Birthday **(JA-pi BER-dei)**

Present **(PRE-zent)**

Cake **(keik)**

El perro (el PEH-ro)

Y (ee)

El gato (el GAH-toh)

El cumpleaños (el koom-play-AHN-yos)

La fiesta (la fee-ES-tah)

La velita (la bay-LEE-tah)

¿Qué? (kay?)

Feliz cumpleaños (fay-LEESE koom-play-AHN-yos)

El regalo (el ray-GAH-loh)

El pastel (el pahs-TEL)